I thought I heard...

For Kitty Clarke

© Aladdin Books Ltd / Alan Baker 1996

Designed and produced by
Aladdin Books Ltd
28 Percy Street
London W1P 0LD

First published in
Great Britain in 1996
Reprinted 1997 by
Aladdin Books / Franklin Watts Books
96 Leonard Street
London EC2A 4RH

Designed by

David West • Children's Books

ISBN 0-7496-2446-9

Printed in Belgium

A CIP catalogue record for this book is
available from the British Library.

I thought I heard...

Alan Baker

ALADDIN/WATTS • LONDON/SYDNEY

I thought I heard a goat's small hooves *tap, tap, tapping* to my door.

It really was...

... a moth's pale wings beating against the window-pane.

I thought I heard the eerie

Whoooooo

of a night-owl in the darkness.

It really was...

... the wild wind whistling down my chimney.

... my bedroom clock ticking away the night.

I thought I heard the

squeak,

squeak

of a huge, grey rat.

It really was...

... the hinges on my creaky bedroom door.

I thought
I heard the

hissss

of a slithery,
slimy snake.
It really was...

... my bubbly water fizzing from its bottle.

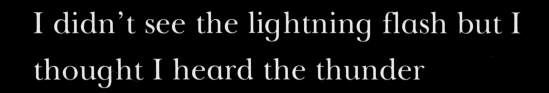

I didn't see the lightning flash but I thought I heard the thunder

crash

It really was...

... my wooden bricks tumbling from the cupboard.

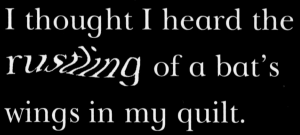

I thought I heard the *rustling* of a bat's wings in my quilt.

It really was...

... my pet cat Kitty, rooting round the rubbish bin.

I thought I heard the

 ₍buzz₎, buzz, buzz

of a giant bumble-bee.

It really was...

... Kitty, purring on my bed.

I thought I heard the soft

meow

of a playful, sleepy cat.

It really was.

Here are the noises I thought I heard.

squeak, squeak

meow

rustling

Whooooooo

crash

click, click, click

tap, tap, tapping

hissss

buzz, buzz, buzz

What were they really?